The Magic Blueberry Bush

Mill City Press, Inc.
2301 Lucien Way #415
Maitland, FL 32751
407.339.4217
www.millcitypress.net

© 2023 by Gabriella Zorzi Ryan

Illustrations by Kateryna Sofishchenko

All rights reserved solely by the author. The author guarantees all contents are original and do not infringe upon the legal rights of any other person or work. No part of this book may be reproduced in any form without the permission of the author.

Due to the changing nature of the Internet, if there are any web addresses, links, or URLs included in this manuscript, these may have been altered and may no longer be accessible. The views and opinions shared in this book belong solely to the author and do not necessarily reflect those of the publisher. The publisher therefore disclaims responsibility for the views or opinions expressed within the work.

Library of Congress Control Number: 2023903307

Paperback ISBN-13: 978-1-66287-216-7
Ebook ISBN-13: 978-1-66287-217-4

Once upon a time, there was a little five-year-old girl named Lia. She lived happily with her mom and dad, her little brother, and their cat.

Lia loved to walk in the woods near her house. She always found interesting plants that her grandmother told her about like bracken ferns, goldenrod flowers, and ladyslippers.

It was a beautiful sunny morning, so Lia decided to go for a short walk in the woods.

The light in the woods was pretty because it came through the spaces between the leaves and made them look like beams casting light in various places on the ground. There was a special beam of light on a beautiful blueberry bush she had never seen before. As Lia looked at the bush, she saw something sparkling within its leaves. There, sitting gracefully on a twig, was a tiny fairy!

The golden pink, glittery fairy fluttered her delicate wings and smiled at Lia.

"Hello, Lia." She spoke in a soft voice that almost sounded like a song.

"How do you know my name?" Lia asked in amazement.

The fairy giggled. "Because I'm magic."

Lia could not believe her discovery. "Magic is real?! What kind of magic can you do?!"

The fairy softly giggled again at the young girl's excitement. "Allow me to introduce myself first. My name is Stelladora, and I can do many things. Though I must say that my favorite kind of magic is when I get to grant three wishes to anyone who finds me. Lia, because you found me in this blueberry bush, I will grant you three wishes. Today, you may tell me your first wish."

Lia thought and thought until the perfect wish finally came to her mind. "I wish to have as many toys as my house can hold!" she shouted.

Suddenly, the wind picked up and rustled the leaves in the trees, followed shortly after by the sound of tinkling bells.

"Bibbidi-Waggle!" Your wish has been fulfilled!" Stelladora exclaimed. "Enjoy your first wish and be sure to visit me next week for your second."

Lia quickly ran out of the woods and back to her house. When she tried to open the door, it wouldn't budge. She looked through the front window and saw her house filled with toys to the very edge of the door!

She managed to pry open the window, and toys of every kind spilled out. There was a rainbow unicorn, a beautiful doll with pretty clothes, a game about castles, puzzles, Play-Doh, slime, and so much more! She had to pull lots of things out just so she could get into the house. Even once she was in, she couldn't move from one room to the other because the toys were taking up all the space!

"Oh, no! This wasn't what I meant!" There were too many different types of toys and she couldn't even decide which one to pick! Even if she could decide, there wasn't any room to play!

Lia heard movement and saw some of the toys shifting. From one of the large piles, her parents, her brother, and her cat crawled out!

"What happened, Lia?!" her father exclaimed. "Where did all of these toys come from?!"

"I found a fairy in a blueberry bush In the woods, who is going to grant me three wishes. This is my first wish, but this isn't what I wanted!"

Lia and her family had to jump out the window just to have some space!

Lia decided to give some of the toys away to her neighbors and friends. Whatever was left she sent to homeless shelters, hospitals, and other places where poorer families could get free things.

Giving the toys away made her feel especially good and, thankfully, Lia and her family could freely walk around their house once more. She realized that she would have to be more careful about her next two wishes.

The next week, Lia went back to the woods and searched for the magic blueberry bush. It was not where it had been before and it took her a while to find it, but another light beam cast a sparkle that caught her eye and led her to it.

"Fairy Stelladora? Are you there?" Lia called as she looked through the leaves.

"Yes, I'm here," a sweet tiny voice answered.

"I think I asked for too much last week," Lia said. "I'm going to be more careful this time."

"Very well, what is your second wish?" Stelladora asked.

"I wish to have as much dessert as my house can hold!" Lia shouted.

The same wind picked up and swept through the woods, followed by the familiar sound of tinkling bells.

"And…Bibbidi-Waggle! Your wish has been fulfilled!" Stelladora exclaimed.

Lia ran home to find the table covered with cakes, ice cream, and other sweets! She was so excited to dig in, but her parents had taught her and her brother they had to eat their supper first before they could eat dessert. She opened the refrigerator to look for some healthy food, but found it was filled with chocolates, pies, cupcakes, cream puffs, jelly donuts, whipped cream, ice cream bars, and many other desserts!

"Lia, what have you wished for now?" her mom asked as she entered the kitchen with her father and brother right behind her. "There's no food left in our house except sweets! I went to the grocery store to buy more food, but as soon as I walked through the door, all of the food turned into desserts!"

Lia explained her second wish and her parents decided to make the most of the sweets that were in the house, but after eating nothing but dessert for a few days, they soon tired of all the sweetness. They craved for other more nourishing foods like fruits, veggies, pasta, and cheese! Even a bowl of cereal in the morning and a nice glass of juice or milk sounded so good!

Lia went to the woods to complain to Stelladora that it wasn't what she meant for that wish. Once again, the blueberry bush had moved to a new spot, so Lia walked around until she found the familiar sparkle.

"Stelladora! You need to undo my second wish!"

The fairy shrugged her tiny shoulders and held up her hands. "I can't undo a wish that has already been granted, but you can."

Lia was surprised. "Really? But how? I don't have magic like you."

Stelladora giggled softly. "Magic is not required, Lia. The only way to undo your wish is to give the desserts away, just like you did with the toys."

Lia happily went home and gave all the sweets to her neighbors and friends. She even had a big dessert party for poorer people who couldn't afford to buy and enjoy tasty treats. Just like when she had given away the toys, she noticed that it made her feel good again when she gave things away.

This gave Lia an idea about her third and final wish. She could not wait and ran back to the magic blueberry bush which, thankfully, had not moved again.

"I'm ready for my last wish, Stelladora," she said excitedly. "I wish that all the people of the world have medicine so they are cared for when they are sick, that they all have good and healthy foods to eat, and that all the children of the world have a few toys to play with!"

The tiny fairy was so happy with Lia's final wish and giggled with joy! One final time, the wind swept through the woods and the tinkling sound was heard.

"And… voila! All of your wishes have been fulfilled," the fairy said with a smile.

"Thank you, Stelladora," Lia said. She blew a kiss to the glittery fairy in the magic blueberry bush before she turned around and ran for home.

When Lia returned, she was so glad that everything was back to normal. She had fun playing with a few toys with her brother in their nice, open living room, before she happily sat and ate a healthy dinner with her family.

"So, Lia, nothing weird has happened today," her little brother said in between bites. "Did you make your last wish?"

"I sure did." Lia smiled and nodded her head, knowing that other families were just as happy as she was.

And they all lived happily ever after.

THE END

"What you keep for yourself, you lose. Only what you give away is what you keep."

by Axel Munthe

CPSIA information can be obtained
at www.ICGtesting.com
Printed in the USA
BVHW012306190623
666128BV00017B/1740